1986
Christopher

Merry Christmas
To My favourite little
Boy.
Love
Aunt Linda

CHARLIE MALARKEY
and the Belly-Button Machine

CHARLIE MALARKEY
and the Belly-Button Machine

BY **WILLIAM** AND **BRENDAN KENNEDY**

ILLUSTRATED BY **GLEN BAXTER**

The Atlantic Monthly Press

Boston · New York

First Edition

LIBRARY OF CONGRESS CATALOGING-IN-PUBLICATION DATA
Kennedy, William, 1928–
    Charlie Malarkey and the belly button machine.
    Summary: When Charlie and his friend Iggy lose
their belly buttons they investigate and discover an
insidious plot to steal and resell belly buttons.
    [1. Belly button—Fiction]   I. Kennedy, Brendan.
II. Baxter, Glen, ill.   III. Title.
PZ7.K3867Ch   1986   [Fic]   86-17291
ISBN 0-87113-104-8

WAK

Published simultaneously in Canada

Typography by Jane Byers Bierhorst
Printed in the United States of America

The authors would like to dedicate this book to
Casey and Shannon Rafferty, two new kids
on the block, of whom the authors are,
respectively, new uncle and
not-so-new grandfather

I look upon it, that he who
does not mind his belly will
hardly mind anything else.

—*Dr. Samuel Johnson*

Authors' Note

Some people may say that the elder author of this story
wrote most of it. This is a very big lie. Partisans of the
younger author may say that he wrote most of it, which is also a
lie, but not such a big one. The fact is that each author, no matter
how much he wrote, wrote exactly fifty percent of everything.
There is no way that either author could have written it
by himself. This is a major truth about this story.

Once upon a time there was a guy named Charlie Malarkey. And once he went to sleep, and when he woke up, there was no belly button on him. He told his mother about it. He said, "I wonder where my belly button went."

His mother lifted up his shirt, and what do you know! His button wasn't there. She said, "Just lie down for a while, Charlie," and she called the doctor. So Charlie went to bed and looked at the place where his belly button used to be and he had a dream that his button was back but that all his toys were gone now. But then he woke up again and he found his toys were really there, but he still didn't have a belly button.

Before the doctor came, Charlie's friend Iggy Gowalowicz came to Charlie's house. Mrs. Malarkey let him in and asked him, "Iggy, do you know where Charlie's belly button went?"

"No," Iggy said, "but I'll help you look for it."

So Charlie and Iggy and Mrs. Malarkey looked first in the book about lost buttons and baby teeth, to find out where to look for lost belly buttons. The book said, "When a belly button is lost, it is usually stolen. Very few people ever lose their belly buttons accidentally. However," said the book, "it is always a good idea to look around the house, just in case."

So everybody looked in the bookcase and in the wastebasket and the garbage can and in the peanut butter jar and under the porch and under Charlie's pillow. But nobody could find it.

Charlie, all of a sudden, grew very angry, and yelled out loudly: "I WANT MY BELLY BUTTON!"

Just then Doctor Mamoluka arrived to give Charlie a checkup.

"Moop," said the doctor, when he got to the place where Charlie's belly button used to be.

"What do you think, Doctor?" Mrs. Malarkey asked.

"Moop," said the doctor, who seemed very upset by the sight of no belly button.

"What do you mean, 'moop'?" said Mrs. Malarkey, who seemed more upset by the doctor than by Charlie's condition. But all the doctor did was give Charlie some quiet medicine.

Charlie asked when he took the medicine, "Will this get me my belly button back?"

But the doctor said only, "Moop," again and foofed out the door.

"'Moop' indeed," said Mrs. Malarkey, and then she went shopping for marmalade meatballs, Charlie's favorite supper. And so Iggy and Charlie were alone in the house when the doorbell rang. Charlie answered the door, and there stood a man with a face like a walnut.

"Hello," said the visitor. "My name is Ben Bubie and I'm in the belly-button business."

"What kind of business is that?" Charlie said.

"I sell belly buttons," said Ben Bubie. "New and used."

"Maybe you could buy one, Charlie," Iggy said.

"How much are they?" Charlie asked the man.

"Five hundred dollars new," said the man. "Twenty-six dollars used. Here's my card. Tell your folks about me."

"If I did get one, how would you put it on me?" Charlie asked.

"I have a machine," Ben Bubie said, and he went down the steps and got into his truck with the lettering on the side that said "Ben Bubie of the Button Box, 246 Abdominable Street." Then he drove away.

"I don't like the looks of that guy," Charlie said. "I bet he knows I lost my belly button."

"How could he know?"

"Maybe he stole it," Charlie said. "Yes, I'll bet he's a belly-button robber."

Iggy's whole body began to twitch. "I'm going home and guard my belly button," he said.

"How are you going to do that?" Charlie asked.

"I don't know. Maybe I'll cover it with my bubble gum."

"Bubble gum doesn't stick," Charlie said. "It comes off on your pajamas. I know what I'd do if I ever thought anybody was going to steal *my* belly button again. I'd cover it over with a Band-Aid and on top of that I'd glue an orange jelly bean to make it look like a belly button."

So Iggy went home, and Charlie put in some very bad hours worrying about what life would be like without a belly button. He tossed in bed all that night and in the morning he wasn't even asleep when the phone rang and it was Iggy, all excited.

"I did what you said," Iggy explained. "I put a jelly bean on top of the Band-Aid and then during the night I thought I dreamed this machine came in my window and stopped right over my belly button. It made a noise and went out and I woke up and looked and the jelly bean was still there, so I knew it was a dream. But then I took the Band-Aid off and THERE WAS NO BELLY BUTTON UNDERNEATH IT."

"This is fantastic," Charlie said. "That machine steals belly buttons right through adhesive tape. If we don't stop this, nobody's belly button will be safe anywhere in the world!"

"We'll call the cops," said Iggy.

"No," said Charlie, "we'll take care of this ourselves. I've got a plan. . . ."

Charlie's plan was to go downtown and find the Button Box and see for himself what kind of place it was. And so he and Iggy walked all the way to 246 Abdominable Street and found it—a three-story building made out of cobblestones, pebbles, marbles, and old golf balls, with a brass doorbell that looked very like a belly button. The round sign over the door said "Ben Bubie's Button Box—Lose A Button? We Can Solve Your Problem." The letters of the sign were made of buttons and the window was also full of buttons, maybe a million of them.

"This Ben Bubie is a button freak," Charlie said. "He's got every kind of button there is."

"Including our belly buttons, I'll bet," Iggy said.

They went around the back of the building and peeked through a window.

"Wow!" said Iggy, "look at that monster." And Charlie came over on his hands and knees and peeked in, and what they both saw was Ben Bubie in his workshop, talking with his assistant (they later found out his name was Marvin Melon). The men were standing in front of a big machine, the likes of which neither boy had ever seen, not even in his nightmares.

"Is that what you thought you saw?" Charlie said.

"No, I never saw that," Iggy said. "But its nose looks familiar."

"Now, Marvin," Ben Bubie was saying to Marvin Melon, who had a head like a small cantaloupe, "this is a dangerous machine that took me twelve years to build, but it was worth it, because it's going to make me rich. Now it's full of electricity, and terrible gas and oil, and smelly acid, and hot pepper, and if you don't handle it just right it can go crazy and ruin all the furniture. So don't push the wrong switch when you are stealing somebody's belly button."

And at that Ben Bubie pushed the "Steal-It-Now" switch and the machine began to work. It was a long, tall, short, thin, fat machine with hairy pipes like legs and arms. It had pancake feet and an enormously long, movable nose (long enough to reach into bedroom windows) that looked like a funnel with the wide side facing out. The machine was made of broken glass and plastic, with cement on one side and very serious wires going in and out of any number of places. At one end it had two unpleasant-looking prongs sticking out of it and the middle was a big tank with eight sides, and rollers and gears and bolts and wing nuts and rivets and springs and several things that looked like lemon doughnuts. It was mostly black, except where it was shocking pink and grisly green, and it had wicked-looking yellow lights that winked like evil eyes. The sound it made was like fingernails scratching on a blackboard and a roomful of giants cracking their knuckles and six hundred and eighty-three chickens squawking and six hundred and eighty-three pigs squealing. And when Ben Bubie turned it on, it smelled like several kinds of cough medicine and Vicks Vapo-Rub and cod-liver oil and broccoli pie with smoked oysters and Charlie and Iggy almost had to leave the backyard.

"That's the most awful thing I've ever seen," Charlie said.

"It smells even worse than that," said Iggy.

"Ben Bubie knows how to do everything that's bad," Charlie said.

Just then the machine began to whistle like a teakettle and blew hot pepper steam out of its two unpleasant prongs. And Charlie and Iggy saw for the first time that a small brown monkey was strapped to a table beside the machine. The monkey was making funny noises and looked quite unhappy. The funnel nose of the machine coiled up like a snake and then hovered right over the monkey's stomach. Then the machine made a definite ploop. "Ploop," it went, and when the funnel snapped back up, the monkey's belly button was gone. The machine then made a muffled pleep. "Pleep," it went, and out of a chute in the great tank a triangular box came sliding.

Ben Bubie opened the box and showed it to Marvin Melon and the two men nodded happily and evilly at what they saw. Ben Bubie wrote "Max b.b." on the box and set it on the shelf. Then he unstrapped Max the monkey and put him in a cage with a second monkey (whose name, the boys would later learn, was Harold).

"Well, the machine is working just fine," Ben Bubie said. "We're all set for another night on the town."

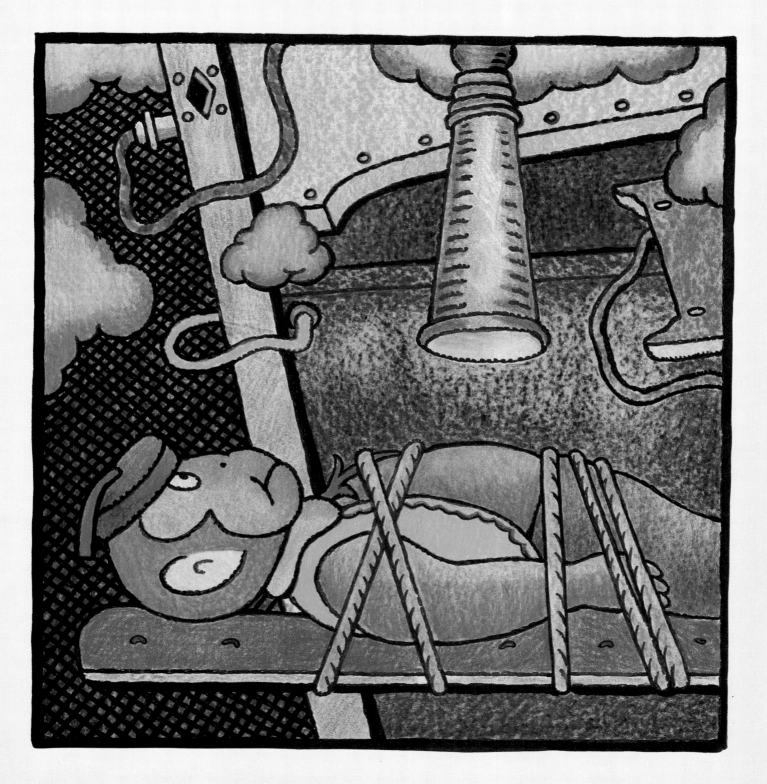

"But we're all out of boxes," Marvin Melon said.

"All out of boxes? All out of boxes?" said Ben Bubie. "You mean to say we're all out of boxes?"

"Yes," said Marvin Melon, "we're all out of boxes. We have no round boxes, no square ones, and we just used the last triangle."

"Why you stoopy goop," said Ben Bubie, "now we have to go out shopping for boxes at a time like this." Ben Bubie then hit Marvin Melon on the ear and knocked him tail over collarbone.

"Get up," he ordered Marvin. "I don't pay you for lying around on the floor."

Charlie and Iggy held their breath at the sight of such nasty business and they breathed easily only when the latch clicked as Ben Bubie and Marvin Melon went out the front door.

"Now," Charlie said, "we'll get a really good look at that machine."

"I'm scared," Iggy said.

"So am I," Charlie said, "but lots of kids will lose their buttons tonight if we don't do something."

Then together they raised the back window, which made a squeak that scared two cats at the other end of the yard. But then it was open, and Charlie and Iggy crawled bravely inside.

Iggy went straight to the cages where Max and Harold were jumping around. Neither monkey had a belly button but neither seemed to mind.

Charlie went to the shelf where a long row of boxes sat alongside a dozen jars of Terrible Oil and Awful Pepper. All the boxes were marked with names, and as he went down the row, Charlie suddenly exploded with excitement. "They're here, Iggy, our buttons are here!"

Charlie opened the round box with "Malarkey" written on it and found it full of mothballs. But in the middle of the mothballs he spotted what looked like a mosquito bite wearing sunglasses. Here's what it looked like:

"There it is," Charlie said. He tried to pick it up but it was slippery and slithered away among the mothballs. Iggy, looking in his box, found the same thing Charlie found, except for the shape of the button, which looked like this:

Iggy looked at Charlie's; then looked at his for a long time without touching it. Then he said, "We'll never get those little things back on where they belong." And he started to cry.

"This is no time for tears," Charlie said. "If that machine is smart enough to take buttons off, it can put them back on again too."

Charlie looked in the middle drawer of the machine and luckily found a book of instructions on how to run what the book called "Ben Bubie's Two-Way Belly Button Projector." The book said: "This machine projects all kinds of belly buttons known to man. It is very good at 'Insies,' and also specializes in 'Outsies.' It will remove belly buttons through anything except dirt. If the target button is buried in dirt, there is no way of getting it away from its owner."

"I wonder why my belly button is all dented," Iggy said.

"Your belly button isn't dented," Charlie said. "It's square."

"Yours isn't square."

"No. Mine is round. That's why it's in a round box."

"In this world everybody has the same belly button."

"Don't be silly," Charlie said. "Some people have belly buttons shaped like noses and knees and others have them shaped like tennis racquets and Popsicles. But this is no time to jibber-jabber about the shape of belly buttons. Are we going to put ours back on or aren't we?"

"No," Iggy said.

"You don't want your button back?"

"I don't like the way it looks."

"It probably looks like it always looked. I'll bet you never really got a good look at it before. Anyway, I'm putting mine on, right now." And Charlie read about how to install belly buttons.

"Make sure," said the book, "that the funnel nose is directly over where the button used to be. This is usually four inches below the front nozzles of the chest bone. Then place the button box, including mothballs, in the 'receiving' section of the 'return platform.' Then have someone press the 'Give-It-Back' switch. It is usually good practice to press the 'Silencer' switch also, so the machine does not make any noise and scare the person you are giving the button back to. If that person moves at the wrong time, an accident could happen."

Charlie put his button box in the receiving section and stretched out on the table. He pulled up his shirt and adjusted the nose of the funnel four inches below his front nozzles.

"Okay," said Charlie, lying very still. "Hit that button, Ig."

When Iggy pushed the "Give-It-Back" switch, the box shlooped inside the machine, which gobbled and wabbled and screeched. Then Charlie felt a very splooking sensation in the middle of his belly. The funnel nose snapped up—spoop!—and Charlie looked down. AND THERE WAS HIS BELLY BUTTON BACK WHERE IT OUGHT TO BE! Sort of.

"It worked, Iggy, see? You want yours on now?"

"Moop," said Iggy.

"'Moop'? What do you mean, 'moop'?"

"Moop," said Iggy, and he stood there. But Charlie convinced him to stretch out on the table, and then ploop, pleep, Iggy too had his button back on. Sort of.

"Now," said Charlie, "we've got to put the buttons back on those monkeys. It's the only decent thing to do." He was strapping Max the monkey on the table when the door slammed open and Ben Bubie rushed in, screaming.

"Why you dirty kids!" he screamed. "Get away from my machine!"

"We know your tricks," Charlie said. "You'll never steal from any more kids in this town. Machines shouldn't have anything to do with kids' belly buttons."

Ben Bubie was so angry he jumped up and down with both feet. His face turned as red as six ripe tomatoes, pink steam shot out of both his ears, and he pointed a ferocious finger at Charlie.

"Why you punk little fathead, I'll take your stupid Irish *nose* away this time!"

Ben Bubie rushed toward Charlie, but Iggy tripped him, and Ben Bubie fell against the machine. Marvin Melon bumbled through the door just then with a load of boxes that almost reached the ceiling. Iggy tripped him, too, and the boxes flew across the room. One hit the "Give-It-Back" switch just as Ben Bubie leaned over the table where Max the monkey was waiting for his belly button. Ben Bubie looked up just as the machine plooped, and the funnel nose came down on his face. When it snapped back up again, Max the monkey's triangle belly button was installed RIGHT AT THE END OF BEN BUBIE'S NOSE!

Harold the monkey opened his cage door by himself just then, jumped onto the machine, and pushed all the buttons. The machine rumbled and rocked, shot hot pepper steam all over the walls and out the windows, played a chorus of "Wabash Cannonball," and then twisted itself into the shape of a poppy-seed bagel.

And Ben Bubie yelled out, "Oh, you dirty, stinking, rotten little kids. You've ruined my machine!"

Marvin Melon, terrified by it all, ran out the door and was never seen again in either North America, Europe, or Asia. Charlie and Iggy grabbed Max and Harold and ran out the door just as the machine gave its last, deep, horrible sound, which went like this:

"Gloumfoumboubleroubledoobleguhziboooo...oh..."

And then the machine went silent and never again did it make a noise. Eventually somebody decided it was a sculpture and it is now on permanent exhibit at the Dead Machinery Museum in Albany, New York.

The boys waited outside and saw Ben Bubie come out, smelling like broccoli and smoked oysters. The police arrived just then and arrested Bubie for disturbing the peace both with his smell and with his nose, which was five times as big as anybody else's nose and kept making noises like a Roman candle.

When Iggy and Charlie got home and took a good look at themselves, they found out they weren't quite the same as they used to be. Iggy's belly button was on sideways, and Charlie's was about an inch too far to the left. This bothered them at first, but they learned to accept it as the price of experience, and in time they even liked the way their belly buttons looked, which was not like anybody else's in the world.

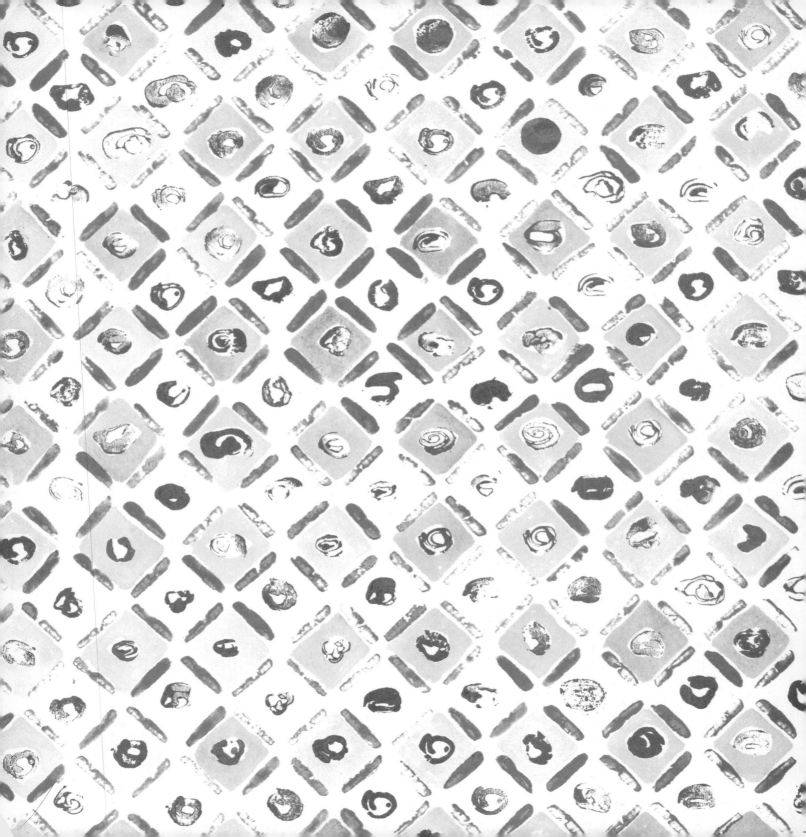